Clifford The BIG RED DOG®

Big New Friend

Clifford created by
Norman Bridwell

Written by
Meredith Rusu

Scholastic Inc.

Copyright © 2021 by Scholastic Entertainment Inc.
CLIFFORD, CLIFFORD THE BIG RED DOG, and associated logos are trademarks and/or registered trademarks of The Norman Bridwell Trust.

PBS KIDS and PBS KIDS logo are trademarks of Public Broadcasting Service. Used with permission.

ISBN 978-1-338-67257-2

10 9 8 7 6

22 23 24 25

Printed in Jefferson City, MO, U.S.A. 40 • First edition 2021

Scholastic Inc., 557 Broadway, New York, NY 10012
Scholastic UK Ltd., Euston House, 24 Eversholt Street, London NW1 1DB
Scholastic LTD, Unit 89E, Lagan Road, Dublin Industrial Estate, Glasnevin, Dublin 11

One morning, Emily Elizabeth and Clifford visited Fisherman Charlie at the docks. They loved hearing his tales of grand adventure out on the deep, blue sea!

"Did I tell ever tell you about the time I almost saw the biggest creature in the world?" Fisherman Charlie asked them.

"Of course," Emily Elizabeth giggled. "Everyone has seen Clifford."

"I'm not talking about Clifford," said Fisherman Charlie. "I'm talking about *Babette*."

"Who's Babette?" asked Emily Elizabeth.

"Why, only the biggest whale in the ocean!" exclaimed Fisherman Charlie. "At least, that's what they say. No one has ever *really* seen her."

"Many years ago, I thought I did," said Fisherman Charlie. "I was whistling a tune on my boat when I heard a splash behind me. I only caught a glimpse of a large white fin before it disappeared."

"I'd love to meet Babette," Clifford told Emily Elizabeth. "It would be nice to have a friend as big as me."

Emily Elizabeth's eyes lit up. "Then we are going to find her!"

Together, they headed to the library to check out some books on whale watching.

When Mrs. Clayton, the librarian, heard their plan, her eyes grew wide.

"Oh, I thought I saw Babette once!" she said. "I was humming a tune on the beach when I spotted a white tail in the water. But it vanished before I could take a closer look."

"Why don't you borrow my binoculars?" Mrs. Clayton offered. "They might help you spot her."

"Wow, thanks!" said Emily Elizabeth.

The friends set off toward the beach on their whale-watching adventure!

Emily Elizabeth read from the library books along the way. "Did you know whales talk to one another by singing?" she asked Clifford.

"I love singing!" Clifford wagged his tail. "Now I *really* hope we find Babette."

On their way, Emily Elizabeth and Clifford passed by her parents.

"We almost saw Babette once," her dad told them when he heard about their mission. "We were dancing to music on the docks when there was a splash behind us. We turned around and thought we saw . . ."

"A big white tail in the water?" guessed Emily Elizabeth.

It seemed like everyone had a story of how they had almost spotted Babette!

"I'm so excited!" said Clifford when they arrived at the beach. "I can't believe I'm finally going to meet someone big just like me!"

"Our whale watch begins—now!" declared Emily Elizabeth.

Clifford and Emily Elizabeth watched.
They waited. And waited.
But they didn't see Babette.

"What if Babette doesn't show up?" Clifford asked, worried.

"There must be a way to find her," insisted Emily Elizabeth. "How did everyone else say they almost saw her?"

"Fisherman Charlie almost saw Babette while he was whistling," Clifford said. "And Mrs. Clayton almost saw her while she was humming."

"And my parents almost saw her while dancing to music," said Emily Elizabeth.

Clifford gasped. "Emily Elizabeth, that's it! Every story has one thing in common—music!"

"You're right!" said Emily Elizabeth. "It's like the book said: whales talk by singing. Maybe if we sing a song, we'll see Babette, too!"

Together, Emily Elizabeth and Clifford sang a tune perfect for a whale.

"WAHHH-EEEE-OOOHHHH-EEEEE-OHHHHH-OHHHH AAAAHH!"

Their idea worked! Two curious eyes poked up above the water.

It was Babette! And the legend was true—she *was* big!

But as soon as Clifford splashed over, Babette dipped back under the waves.

"I think she's shy," Clifford realized. "Maybe *that's* why no one has ever seen her."

So, Clifford sang a song to help her feel less nervous.

"I've always been larger than everyone else, you see,
and I have to admit, at times, it's lonely.
But not today! I'm as happy as can be.
It feels so good to know someone as big as me!"

Clifford's song worked! Babette popped out of the ocean.
She was excited to meet someone the same size as her, too!

"We did it, Emily Elizabeth!" cried Clifford. "We found Babette!"

"And you found a new friend," Emily Elizabeth said happily.

Clifford grinned from ear to ear. "A big new friend!"

USA • PO# 5072745• 02/22